WHAT DO BUNNIES DO ALL DAY?

Written and Illustrated by
Judy Mastrangelo

IDEALS CHILDREN'S BOOKS

Nashville, Tennessee

To Bunny
For all of his love and help
in making this book

Printed and bound in the United States of America.
Published by Ideals Publishing Corporation
Nelson Place at Elm Hill Pike
Nashville, Tennessee 37214

ISBN 0-8249-8311-4

"Is it time yet?" asked Little Bunny.

Mother Bunny smiled. The air smelled of
sweet new grass, and the warm sun made her
soft fur shine. It was a perfect spring day.

"But what shall I do all day by myself?" asked
Little Bunny. "What do bunnies do all day?"

It felt very strange not to have Mother Bunny
close-by, but it was all very exciting.

As Little Bunny sat in the meadow nibbling dandelions, he gazed up at the blue sky.

A fluffy, white cloud floated above him.
"Hello, little cloud!" the bunny cried out.
"What do you do all day?"

"How wonderful!" shouted Little Bunny. "I can have a whole day to myself. I can do whatever I want." He hopped up and down and happily rolled over and over.

"All right," said Mother Bunny as she nuzzled
her little bunny. "I suppose it's time. You're old
enough now. Just be back at suppertime."

The friendly cloud answered, "I sail all through the bright blue sky. When I look down, I can see many lands and cities and lakes and rivers."

"Oh, what fun!" exclaimed the little rabbit.
"But how is it that you move so fast?"

"Why, my friend the wind blows me,"
answered the cloud. "See, I'm sailing away now.
Good-by-y-y-ye."

"I'm not light enough to float in the sky," called
Little Bunny as he waved good-bye to the cloud.

He hopped on until he came to a clump of
bright yellow spring flowers. Little Bunny stood
tall on his tippytoes and spoke to a big daffodil.
"Good afternoon, pretty flower. Could you

please tell me what you do all day?"

"Why, hello, little rabbit," she said. "We daffodils feel the bright warm sun on our faces all day."

"But don't you go anywhere to see anybody?"
asked Little Bunny.

"No," she answered, "but we don't get lonely.
We have lots of other flowers to talk to. The
earth and grass are wonderful company, and
we have many visitors who come each day to
tell us of news beyond our field."

Just then Little Bunny saw two butterflies and a bee who came to visit the flowers. The bee even told him how he gathered pollen from the flowers to bring it back to make his honey.

"Well, I can see that flowers are never lonely," said the bunny, "but I don't think I could do what flowers do all day. I couldn't stay in one place for very long." Thanking the flowers, Little Bunny hopped away.

Little Bunny felt very hungry. Just then he spied something red, sweet, and very juicy-looking.

"Yummm, raspberries," he said, as he hopped over to nibble his fill.

He then washed his little face and ears and
feet and fur in the warm sun. "I know what

clouds and flowers do now," he said, "but what do bunnies do all day?"

Little Bunny was very sleepy. He found a
small shady spot, yawned and stretched, then
curled up in a little furry ball under a bush.
Soon he was fast asleep.

When he awoke, he felt very thirsty. He came
to a stream where he licked up some clear cool
water. After drinking, he said to the stream,
"Please, bubbling stream, can you tell me what
you do all day?"

"Many forest creatures come here to drink, just like you, Little Bunny. Later, deer and other animals will visit and I'll give them a cool evening drink."

"Thank you for the drink," said Little Bunny,
"but I must hurry home now. It's almost
suppertime."

When he arrived home, his mother asked,
"Well, Little Bunny, what did you do all day?"

"I hopped and I skipped and I jumped. I nibbled dandelions, washed in the warm sun, took a nap, ate raspberries, and sipped cool water from a stream. But," said Little Bunny sadly, "I never did find out what bunnies do all day."

"What bunnies do all day is exactly what my Little Bunny did," said Mother Bunny as she hugged him tightly. Then they ate their supper and went to bed.